no exceptions

By Eleanor Robins

SADDLEBACK
EDUCATIONAL PUBLISHING

C H O I C E S

Break All Rules

Broken Promise

Don't Get Caught

Double-Cross

Easy Pass

Friend or Foe?

No Exceptions

No Limits

Pay Back

Trust Me

SADDLEBACK
EDUCATIONAL PUBLISHING
www.sdlback.com

ISBN-13: 978-1-61651-597-3
ISBN-10: 1-61651-597-X
eBook: 978-1-61247-243-0

Printed in Malaysia

21 20 19 18 17   6 7 8 9 10

Meet the Characters from

no exceptions

Malik: Tyler's friend, does not finish his paper over the weekend, drives Tyler to school, feels sorry for Darcie

Tyler: Malik's friend, wants to turn his paper in late, thinks Darcie is rude

Darcie: smart girl who gets As and always turns in her assignments on time

Mr. Li: English teacher at the high school

chapter 1

It was Monday morning. Malik was on his way to school. He was in his car.

Malik was on his way to pick up his friend Tyler. Then Malik would drive them both to school.

Malik got to Tyler's house. And he honked the horn.

The front door of the house opened. And Tyler came out of the house. He hurried to the car. And he got in the car. Then he looked over at Malik.

Tyler said, "Don't get me in trouble."

"What are you talking about?" Malik asked.

"You honked the horn. And that makes my dad and mom mad," Tyler said.

"Sorry. But you weren't outside. And I don't want to be late to school," Malik said.

"Just please don't do it again. You know I'll be right out. You don't have to honk the horn, dude," Tyler said.

"Okay, I won't honk the horn next time. But be sure you come right out. So I won't need to do it," Malik said.

"I will," Tyler said.

The boys rode for a few minutes. And they didn't talk.

Then Tyler said, "Did you finish your term paper last night?"

"No, did you?" Malik asked.

"No," Tyler said.

The boys were in the same English

class. And they had term papers due the next day. They both had said they'd finish their papers over the weekend. They didn't want to work on them Monday night.

"On Friday, you said you were going to finish your paper this weekend. So you wouldn't have to do it tonight," Malik said.

"I know I said that. But you said the same thing. And you didn't finish your paper," Tyler said.

The boys rode for a few more minutes. And they didn't talk.

Then Malik said, "Why didn't you finish your paper?"

Tyler said, "No good reason. I guess because I didn't want to work on it last night."

"The same with me," Malik said.

"We didn't finish our papers. So you

know what that means," Tyler said.

"We have to stay up tonight until we finish them. And that means very late for me," Malik said.

"The same for me. And now I wish I'd done it over the weekend," Tyler said.

"But it's too late for us to think about that," Malik said.

The two boys rode for a few more minutes. And they didn't talk.

Then Tyler said, "I might ask Mr. Li if we can wait until Friday. And turn our papers in then."

Mr. Li was their English teacher.

"You know what Mr. Li will say," Malik said.

Tyler said, "I know. You'll get a zero if you don't turn your paper in tomorrow."

"You've got that right. That's what he'll say," Malik said.

"But I still think I'll ask Mr. Li. He

won't give me a zero for asking," Tyler said.

Malik said, "I wouldn't do it. But ask him if you want to. But we know what he'll say."

"I still think I'll ask him. We don't know for sure what he'll say," Tyler said.

"This time I think we do," Malik said.

"But I don't want to stay up late tonight. So I still think I'll ask him," Tyler said again.

"Maybe by class time you'll change your mind about that," Malik said.

"Maybe," Tyler said.

Malik didn't think Mr. Li would let them wait until Friday. And he didn't think Tyler should ask Mr. Li to let them do that.

But Malik didn't want to stay up late and write his paper either. So in a way he wished Tyler would ask Mr. Li.

chapter
2

It was the same morning. Malik was in his English class. Tyler was there too. It was almost time for class to start.

Malik looked over at Tyler. Tyler sat next to him.

Malik said, "What are you going to do? Are you going to ask if we can turn our papers in Friday? And not tomorrow?"

"Yes," Tyler said.

Malik didn't think Tyler should ask that. But he was glad that Tyler was going to ask it. There was always a

11

chance Mr. Li would let them wait until Friday. But Malik was sure Mr. Li wouldn't do that.

The bell rang to start class.

Mr. Li called the roll. Then he said, "Are there any questions before we start the lesson?"

Tyler quickly raised his hand.

Mr. Li looked at Tyler.

"Yes, Tyler," said Mr. Li. "What is your question?"

"Can we wait until Friday to turn in our papers?" Tyler asked.

Mr. Li just looked at Tyler. He didn't look pleased. And he didn't say anything.

Malik could tell that he didn't like it that Tyler asked that.

A girl quickly raised her hand. And she began to wave it around. Mr. Li would be sure to see she had her hand up.

She sat in the desk in front of Malik.

And her name was Darcie.

Mr. Li looked at Darcie.

"Yes, Darcie," Mr. Li said. "Can your question wait until after I answer Tyler's question?"

"I don't have a question. I just want to say something about what Tyler said," Darcie said.

"What would you like to say about it, Darcie?" Mr. Li asked.

"You told the class that we had to turn our papers in tomorrow. And we all know that. And we all had plenty of time to write our papers," Darcie said.

Malik hoped Darcie wouldn't say anything else. But she did.

"The rest of us aren't like some people in the class," Darcie said.

And Malik knew the whole class knew she was talking about Tyler. And Mr. Li knew she was too.

Darcie said, "Some of us plan ahead. And we do all of our work on time. But some people are lazy. And they wait until the last minute to do things. And they shouldn't get extra time to do their work."

Then she leaned back in her desk. And she folded her arms.

Mr. Li looked back at Tyler.

Then he said, "You know your paper is due tomorrow, Tyler. And Darcie is right. You had plenty of time to do it. Turn it in tomorrow. Or you will get a zero. I won't grade papers that are turned in late."

Mr. Li got his English textbook off of his desk. Then he said, "Open your books, class. And turn to page ninety. It is time to start the lesson."

Malik and Tyler quickly opened their English books. And they turned to page 90.

Then Tyler looked over at Malik. He said, "I wish Darcie would keep her mouth shut."

But only Malik could hear what he said.

Malik knew Tyler wasn't mad about what Mr. Li said. But he was mad at Darcie.

Malik wasn't mad at Darcie. But he didn't like what she said. Tyler was right. She should have kept her mouth shut.

chapter 3

It was the same morning. Malik was still in his English class.

The end of class bell rang.

Mr. Li said, "Have a good day, class. And don't forget that your papers are due tomorrow."

Malik didn't think any of the students could forget that. Not after what Tyler and Darcie had said. And after what Mr. Li had said to Tyler.

Mr. Li said, "And you must turn your papers in tomorrow. Or you will get a zero. I won't grade late papers. And don't forget I told you that."

Darcie said, "And you shouldn't grade late papers, Mr. Li. We've all had plenty of time to write them."

Then Darcie turned around. And she looked at Tyler. She said, "Don't forget your paper is due tomorrow."

Malik didn't think she said it to be nice to Tyler. But maybe he was wrong about that.

Tyler said, "Mind your own business, Darcie. And stay out of mine."

Darcie looked at him. And she looked mad. Then she said, "That was rude." And she turned around.

Darcie quickly got her books. And she hurried out of the room.

Malik said, "That was rude, Tyler."

"So what? She should mind her own business," Tyler said.

"She's nosey. But she's one pretty girl," Malik said.

"She's pretty. But that doesn't make up for her being rude. And being in everyone's business," Tyler said.

"You're right about that," Malik said.

"I wish she wasn't in our classes," Tyler said.

Darcie was in three of their classes. And she acted the same in all three classes.

"At least she isn't in our math class. So we can be glad about that," Malik said.

Tyler said, "You're right. That's something good. She has math first. And she sits in the same desk as me. And sometimes she leaves some of her junk in it. And it's in my way when I go to class."

Tyler had told Malik that before. And Malik knew Tyler didn't like it when Darcie did that.

Tyler picked up his books. And he started to go. Then he looked at Malik.

"You don't think I made Mr. Li mad, do you?" Tyler said. "Because I asked about the paper."

"No, I don't think so," Malik said.

"Maybe I should talk to him before I leave," Tyler said. Then he hurried over to Mr. Li. He told Mr. Li he didn't mean to be rude.

Mr. Li said, "I know students like to put things off, Tyler. I was a student once myself. And students back then wanted to put things off too. And I was one of those who felt that way."

"You were?" Tyler said. He sounded surprised.

"Yes, Tyler. But you can't do that in my class. Now hurry on to where you should go now," said Mr. Li. "Or you'll be late."

Tyler hurried out the door. And so did Malik.

Malik was glad Darcie had already gone. And she wasn't in the room to say something about what Tyler said.

chapter 4

It was the next morning. Malik was on his way to his English class. Tyler was walking with him.

Malik said, "I sure am tired."

"So am I. I wish I had done my paper over the weekend. And not had to finish it last night. I wanted to go to bed. And I thought I'd never finish it," Tyler said.

"I guess Darcie was right. We should've planned ahead. And not waited until the last minute to finish our papers," Malik said.

"Don't say that. And don't even think that. Darcie is never right," Tyler said.

But they both knew Darcie was right. They should have done their papers sooner.

The two boys got to the door of their classroom. Tyler stopped walking.

That surprised Malik. He stopped walking too. "Why did you stop?" he asked.

"I know I have my paper. But I want to make real sure that I do," Tyler said.

Tyler quickly looked to make sure he had his paper. Then he said, "I have it."

The two boys started to walk into the classroom.

Malik was tired. And he didn't watch where he was going. He bumped into Darcie. But he didn't mean to do it.

Darcie glared at him. She said, "Why did you bump into me?"

"I'm sorry. I didn't mean to do it. I'm just tired. And I didn't watch where I was going," Malik said.

"No wonder you're tired. I bet you had to finish your paper last night. And you had to stay up late to do it," Darcie said.

Malik thought about telling Darcie she was wrong. But he knew she wouldn't believe him. So he might as well tell her the truth.

"You're right. That's why I'm tired. I had to stay up late to finish my paper," Malik said.

"It's all your fault that you're tired," Darcie said.

"I know that, Darcie. You don't have to tell me that," Malik said. He was starting to get mad at Darcie.

"You should've done your paper sooner. And not at the last minute. Then you would've gotten enough sleep last night,"

Darcie said.

Tyler said, "Mind your own business, Darcie."

Malik knew that would make Darcie mad. And he wished Tyler hadn't said that to her.

Darcie glared at Tyler. She said, "I wasn't talking to you."

Then Darcie went into the classroom. And she walked over to her desk. And she sat down.

Malik was glad Darcie had quit talking to him.

Tyler was right. Darcie should mind her own business.

And Malik wished she wasn't in the class. Or in his other classes. And he wished he didn't feel that way about her. But at least she wasn't in all of his classes.

Tyler said, "Just once I wish Darcie

would forget to do her homework. Or leave it at home. Or something. So she would get a bad grade."

"You shouldn't feel that way, Tyler," Malik said.

"I know. But I do," Tyler said.

Malik felt the same way about Darcie. And he wished he didn't. But he didn't have to feel bad about what he thought. Because there was one thing he knew about Darcie for sure. She would never forget to do her homework. And she always turned in her homework and papers on time.

chapter 5

Darcie had gone into the classroom. But Malik and Tyler were still in the hall.

Malik said, "We need to get in the classroom, dude. It is almost time for class to start."

"I know. But I wish Darcie wasn't in there. I hope she doesn't say anything else to me," Tyler said.

Malik hoped she didn't either. And he hoped Tyler didn't say anything else to Darcie.

Malik went into the classroom. Tyler was right behind him.

The two boys hurried over to their desks. And they sat down.

Darcie was still at her desk. And Malik was glad she didn't say anything else to them.

The bell rang to start class.

Mr. Li got up from his desk. And he quickly called the roll.

Then Mr. Li said, "Time to turn in your papers. Pass them to the person at the front of your row."

Malik quickly got out his paper. And Tyler got out his too.

Malik tried to pass his paper up to Darcie. But Darcie didn't take it. She was looking for her paper.

Malik said, "Here, Darcie. Take my paper."

But Darcie didn't take it. And she

kept looking for her paper. Then she said, "Oh, no."

Mr. Li looked over at Darcie. He said, "Is something wrong, Darcie?"

"I can't find my paper. I know I brought it to school. But I can't find it," Darcie said.

Tyler leaned over. And he tapped Malik on the arm.

Malik turned to look at him. Tyler had a big smile on his face.

Malik knew Tyler was glad Darcie couldn't find her paper.

Darcie was still busy looking through all of her things.

Mr. Li said, "Darcie is busy looking for her paper, Malik. Please bring your paper to the person at the front of your row."

Malik quickly got up. He walked to the front of his row. And he gave his paper to Brooklyn who sat in front.

Then Malik went back to his desk. And he sat down.

Mr. Li said, "Darcie, I need your paper."

Darcie was the only student who hadn't turned a paper in.

"I can't find it. But I'm sure I brought it to school. Can I turn it in tomorrow?" Darcie asked.

Malik couldn't believe Darcie asked Mr. Li that question.

Darcie said, "I must have lost my paper. I can print out another copy of it tonight. And I can bring it tomorrow."

Tyler said, "You can't do that. Mr. Li said we had to turn our papers in today. Or we would get a zero."

Darcie turned around. And she looked at Tyler. She looked very mad. She said, "I asked Mr. Li. Not you."

Tyler said, "You had plenty of time

to write your paper. So you should have had it done by today."

Darcie looked even madder. And her face was very red. "I did do my paper. I just can't find it," she said. She almost yelled the words at Tyler.

"How do we know you did? You don't have your paper," Tyler said.

Mr. Li said, "That's enough, Tyler."

Darcie said, "Please, Mr. Li. Let me turn my paper in tomorrow. I promise you that I did it. And I brought it to school this morning. But I don't know where it is."

"I'm sorry, Darcie. You have until the end of the day to find it. And turn it in to me. Or else you'll get a zero," Mr. Li said. "No exceptions."

All of the other students had turned their papers in. And Mr. Li put all of the papers on top of his desk.

Then Mr. Li said, "Get out your English books, class. It's time to start the lesson."

Malik looked over at Tyler. Tyler still had a big smile on his face.

Malik knew Tyler was glad Darcie couldn't find her paper. But Malik felt sorry for her.

Darcie always got the best grade on her work. She had to find her paper before school was out. Or else she would get a zero. And that would hurt her grade point average. And she wouldn't get an A in English on her report card.

chapter 6

Malik was still in his English class. It was almost time for class to be over. Mr. Li was talking to the students about their homework.

Malik had hoped they wouldn't have any homework. But he should have known they would. Mr. Li gave them homework at least four days a week.

Mr. Li said, "Do you have any questions? Now is the time to ask them."

Three students raised their hands. And Mr. Li answered their questions.

Then Malik raised his hand.

Mr. Li said, "Yes, Malik. Do you have a question about the homework?"

"No, Mr. Li. It is about our papers," Malik said.

"What about your papers?" Mr. Li asked.

"When do you think we'll get them back? So we can find out what we got on them," Malik said.

Malik hoped he did well on his paper. And he thought he did. So he was in a hurry to find out what he got on it.

Mr. Li said, "I'll grade your papers as soon as I can. But I won't have a chance to finish them until this weekend. I'll plan to give them back to you on Monday."

The end of class bell rang.

"Have a good day, class," Mr. Li said.

Tyler looked at Malik. He said, "I didn't know teachers had to do schoolwork on the weekends."

"That was news to me too. I hope Mr. Li doesn't give us work to do this weekend," Malik said.

"I hope not too. We had enough to do for his class last weekend," Tyler said.

"But we didn't do it. We waited until last night to do it," Malik said.

Then Malik stood up. And he looked at Darcie.

Darcie still looked very upset. And Malik still felt sorry for her.

"Maybe you didn't bring your paper to school this morning, Darcie," said Malik. "Are you sure you brought it? Maybe you should call home. And see if you left your paper there."

Darcie glared at him. She said, "What do you think I am? Stupid? I know I brought my paper to school this morning. And I didn't leave it at home."

"I didn't mean you were stupid. I just meant maybe you just thought you brought your paper today. And you didn't. I have left things at home before. And thought I brought them to school," Malik said.

"Well, I'm not you," Darcie said.

Tyler said, "That's for sure. Malik is nice. And you aren't. You are one rude girl."

"And what do you think you are?" Darcie said. She almost yelled the words at Tyler.

"Not like you. That's for sure," Tyler said.

Mr. Li walked over to them. He said, "Is there a problem here, students?"

"No, Mr. Li. We're just getting ready to go to lunch," Malik said.

Tyler and Darcie didn't say anything.

Malik quickly picked up his books.

And he started towards the door. Tyler was right behind him.

The two boys walked out into the hall.

Darcie walked out the door behind them. But she didn't say anything to them. And they didn't say anything to her.

It was time for Malik and Tyler to go to lunch. And they walked to the lunchroom.

chapter 7

The two boys got to the lunchroom. They went into the lunchroom. And they got their lunches. Then they walked over to a table. And they sat down.

Tyler said, "I still can't believe Darcie didn't bring her paper today."

"I know. That's hard to believe. Why do you think she didn't bring it?" Malik asked.

"I don't know. Maybe she hasn't written it yet," Tyler said.

"I know you don't believe that," Malik said.

"No, I don't. I guess Darcie forgot it. And she left it at home. And she didn't want us to know she forgot it," Tyler said.

"Maybe. But maybe she lost it some-where at school," Malik said.

"Maybe. But I still think she left it at home. And she didn't want us to know she forgot it," Tyler said.

The two boys ate for a few minutes. And they didn't talk.

Then Tyler said, "Do you know how to do our English homework?"

"I think so. Do you?" Malik asked.

Tyler said, "I think so. But I'm not sure I do. I guess I'll find out tonight when I start to do it."

The two boys ate for a few more minutes.

Then Tyler said, "Maybe Darcie will leave that homework at home too. And she'll get another zero."

"Maybe Darcie will find her paper

before school is out. And then she won't get a zero on it," Malik said.

"I hope she doesn't find it," Tyler said.

"You shouldn't feel that way, Tyler," Malik said.

But Malik knew why Tyler felt that way. And he didn't blame Tyler for feeling that way. Darcie had been very rude to Tyler. And to him too.

Tyler said, "Darcie should make a zero. She's always so rude."

"She isn't rude all of the time," Malik said.

"Maybe she isn't. But it sure seems like she is," Tyler said.

Darcie walked by their table. She looked at the two boys. Then she said, "I know you two are talking about me. Stop it."

"Why would we talk about you? We have better things to talk about than you. And we wrote our papers. You didn't write your paper," Tyler said.

"I did write it," Darcie said.

"How do we know you wrote it? You can't prove you did," Tyler said.

"I brought my paper to school. And I lost it," Darcie said.

"Students always say that when they don't do their work," Tyler said.

"I'm not like other students," Darcie said.

"You're right about that. Other students aren't rude like you are," Tyler said.

Darcie looked very mad. She quickly walked to a table on the other side of the lunchroom. And she sat down.

"That was rude, Tyler," Malik said.

"I know. But I couldn't help it. She makes me so mad. And she said we were talking about her," Tyler said.

"We were talking about her," Malik said.

"But she didn't know for sure that we were," Tyler said.

The boys ate for a few more minutes.

Then Malik said, "I feel sorry for Darcie."

Tyler looked surprised by what Malik said.

"Why do you feel sorry for Darcie?" Tyler asked.

"Because she has to find her paper before school is out. Or else she'll get a zero. And Darcie always does well. And a zero will hurt her grade," Malik said.

"Too bad," Tyler said.

But Tyler didn't look like he thought it was too bad. And he didn't sound like he thought it was.

"It is too bad. We both know Darcie did her paper. She doesn't have to prove it to us. She always does her work. And she always turns it in on time," Malik said.

"Not today," Tyler said.

"But you know she did her paper," Malik said.

"I believe she did it. And maybe she did lose it at school," Tyler said.

"Then she shouldn't get a zero. And I hope she finds her paper before school is out. So she can turn it in to Mr. Li," Malik said.

"I hope she doesn't find it," Tyler said.

Malik said, "It could have been one of us who lost our paper. And we could be the ones who will get a zero."

"But we didn't lose our papers. Darcie did. And I'm glad she'll get a zero," Tyler said.

Malik didn't think he could change Tyler's mind about that. So he didn't say anything else to Tyler about Darcie.

chapter 8

It was the same day. The boys left the lunchroom. And they started to walk to their math class.

Darcie walked by them. But she didn't say anything to them. And Malik was glad she didn't.

Tyler said, "I sure am glad Darcie isn't in our next class."

Malik was glad too.

Tyler said, "You feel sorry for Darcie. So I guess you wish she was in the class with us."

"Not me. Three classes a day with Darcie is enough for me. I'm glad she's in first period math class. And not in our class with us," Malik said.

The boys got to their classroom. And they went into the room. They walked over to their desks. And they sat down.

Tyler started to put some of his things in his desk. Then he laughed. And he got a big smile on his face.

"Why are you laughing?" Malik asked.

"Guess what I found," Tyler said.

"What?" Malik asked.

Tyler took a lot of papers out of his desk. And he waved them at Malik.

Tyler said, "I found Darcie's lost paper. She left it in here when she had this class."

"Darcie will be very happy when you give it to her," Malik said.

And he was glad Tyler found it.

"I'm not going to give it to her," Tyler said.

That surprised Malik. "Why not?" he asked.

Tyler said, "Because Darcie is so rude. And because she said people shouldn't get extra time to do their work."

"But Darcie did her work," Malik said.

"But she didn't have it in class today," Tyler said.

"What are you going to do with her paper?" Malik asked. He hoped Tyler didn't plan to throw it away.

Tyler said, "I'll leave it in this desk. And Darcie will find it tomorrow morning when she has this class."

"But it'll be too late for her to find it then. And she'll get a zero," Malik said.

"Too bad," Tyler said.

But Malik knew Tyler didn't really mean that.

"You have to give it to her, Tyler," Malik said.

"Why?" Tyler asked.

"Think of how you'd feel if you lost your paper. And Darcie found it. And she didn't give it to you," Malik said.

"Darcie wouldn't give me my paper if she found it," Tyler said.

"You don't know that, Tyler. And I think she would. She might be rude. But she isn't mean," Malik said.

At first, Tyler didn't say anything.

But then Tyler said, "I guess you're right. I guess she would give it to me if she found it. But I'm not sure she would."

"I'm sure she would," Malik said. And he was sure Darcie would.

Tyler said, "Darcie has been too rude to me. So I won't give her paper to her. But you can give it to her if you want to do it."

"Okay," Malik said.

Tyler handed Darcie's term paper to Malik.

Malik said, "It's almost time for class to start. So it's too late to find Darcie now. But I'll give this to her as soon as class is over. And she can take it to Mr. Li."

Then Darcie would be able to get a good grade.

Malik would be nice to Darcie. And maybe Darcie would start being nicer to other people. But Malik wasn't sure she would be.

But it didn't matter. Malik would still give Darcie's paper to her. That's what he would want someone else to do for him.

consider
this...

1. Have you ever done something at the last minute?

2. How would you respond to Darcie if she was rude to you?

3. Have you ever asked a teacher if you could turn an assignment in late?

4. Did you ever do the right thing even though you didn't want to?

5. Was Tyler wrong for not wanting to help Darcie?